The
Frightened
Kitten

Other titles by Holly Webb:

Lost in the Snow

Lost in the Storm

Alfie all Alone

Sam the Stolen Puppy

Max the Missing Puppy

Sky the Unwanted Kitten

Timmy in Trouble

Ginger the Stray Kitten

Harry the Homeless Puppy

Buttons the Runaway Puppy

Alone in the Night

Ellie the Homesick Puppy

Jess the Lonely Puppy

Misty the Abandoned Kitten

Oscar's Lonely Christmas

Lucy the Poorly Puppy

Smudge the Stolen Kitten

The Rescued Puppy

The Kitten Nobody Wanted

The Lost Puppy

The Frightened Kitten

Holly Webb

Illustrated by Sophy Williams

For Lara

For more information about Holly Webb visit:
www.holly-webb.com

STRIPES PUBLISHING
An imprint of Magi Publications
1 The Coda Centre, 189 Munster Road,
London SW6 6AW

A paperback original
First published in Great Britain in 2012

Text copyright © Holly Webb, 2012
Illustrations copyright © Sophy Williams, 2012

ISBN: 978-1-84715-230-5

A CIP catalogue record for this book is available
from the British Library.

Printed and bound in the UK.

10 9 8 7 6 5 4 3 2 1

Chapter One

"Make sure you wrap it up carefully," Kate told Maddy, stuffing an armful of bubble wrap into her best friend's lap.

Maddy nodded, smoothing it out and starting to wind it round the photo frame. "Ben looks gorgeous in this picture," she said, her voice a bit wobbly.

Kate nodded. "He always does. But that's my favourite photo of him."

Maddy stared down at the photo – she was in it too. It had been taken last summer, and showed her and Kate, with Kate's huge black cat Ben sitting on the picnic rug between them. He was almost as tall as they were, when the girls were sitting down.

She laughed with surprise as a hard head butted her arm, and Ben stomped his way on to her lap to see exactly what she was doing. He'd been asleep at the end of Kate's bed, but he'd obviously decided something interesting was happening. He was the world's nosiest cat.

"Do you think he'll mind moving?" Maddy asked, watching Kate fill a big cardboard box with books and her ornaments, all carefully wrapped up.

"I do
new h
likes
mis
to
m

leaving to
for that." She smi
next to Maddy and Ben on th

Maddy put an
Ben bounced o
up on his hi
paws arou
trick. K
a cat
do

arm round her, and
n to Kate's lap, standing
nd legs to wrap his front
d her neck. It was his party
ate always told people she had
who hugged, although he didn't
it to very many people. Mostly
ate, but he would do it to Maddy
sometimes, especially if she'd given
him a cat treat. He'd even done it to
Maddy's dad once, when he came to
pick Maddy up and stopped for a cup
of tea. Her dad had been taken by
surprise, but Maddy had noticed that
he always looked for Ben whenever he
came to Kate's now. As though he was
hoping that Ben might do it again.

Maddy had been working on her
mum and dad to let her get a cat of

her own for ages. She was pretty sure that Ben had won her dad over that day. Now she just had to persuade her mum…

Kate sniffed again. "What if he doesn't like the new house, Maddy? He might even try and find his way back here. You read in the papers about cats who do that."

"Yorkshire's probably too far for him to try it," Maddy said. It was meant to be comforting, but it didn't work. She didn't want to think about how far away her friend was going to be. And she was going to have to start a new school, of course. Maddy couldn't imagine having to do that.

Kate frowned. "I hope there aren't too many other cats near the new house.

Ben's the top cat round here, none of the other cats would put a paw in our garden. But the new garden might be another cat's territory already."

Maddy looked down at Ben, now sitting comfortably on Kate's lap. He yawned and stretched, and then stared up at her with huge green eyes. *He* didn't look like he was worried.

"Even if the garden is another cat's territory, I don't think it will be for long," Maddy said, stroking him.

Kate nodded, laughing. "Maybe. He doesn't fight very often, but when he does, I think he just sits on the other cats and squashes them." She sighed. "I suppose I'd better get on with packing. Mum says I should have had it finished yesterday." She pushed Ben gently off her knee, and he slunk away to hide among the boxes.

Maddy went back to wrapping up the photo. She was going to miss Kate so much. She knew Kate would miss her too, but her friend was a bit like Ben, Maddy thought. She was so strong and bouncy and confident. She'd have a new gang of friends in no time – and she'd be showing off her famous hugging cat to them instead.

"Pass me that tape, Maddy, so I can seal this box up."

Maddy handed her the parcel tape, and wrapped another photo frame. "Where did Ben go?" she asked, a few minutes later.

"He's under the bed, isn't he?" Kate said, peering down.

But he wasn't. There was a sudden thumping and then a muffled yowl. "He's in the box!" Maddy giggled.

Kate stared at the big cardboard box she'd just taped up. "He can't be…" she murmured, but she didn't sound very sure. She ripped off the tape, and the flaps came up, followed by a large black head, with cross, glowing green eyes. Ben scrambled out, hissing grumpily.

"Well, you shouldn't have been in there!" Kate laughed. "Nosy boy!"

Maddy was laughing too. But even as she laughed, she was thinking, *I'm going to miss them so much…*

Kate and her mum walked Maddy home – it was only five minutes away, and it was warm and sunny. Perfect Easter holiday weather. If Kate hadn't been leaving tomorrow, they'd have spent loads of time in the park, or maybe gone out somewhere for the day.

"Those cats that live next door to you are nearly as big as Ben," Kate's mum commented, as they came up to Maddy's garden.

"They're sitting on Mum's daffodils again," Maddy sighed, as she hurried into the front garden and tried to shoo the two big ginger cats off the stone pot that her mum had planted full of bulbs. For some reason Tiger and Tom had decided it was a really good place to sit, and the daffodils were looking a bit squashed now.

Maddy's mum opened the front door. "I heard you coming, girls. Oh, no, not those horrible cats again!"

Tiger spat crossly at Maddy as she tried to get him off the daffodils, and yowled. He was so different to lovely, sweet-natured Ben. At last, he jumped down, and the pair of them stalked away, glaring back at Maddy.

As the mums chatted, Kate flung her arms round Maddy. "Promise you'll call me every day! Tell me everything that's happening at school, OK?"

Maddy nodded. "And anyway, you're coming back to visit at half-term."

"We'd better go," Kate's mum said. "It'll be a long day tomorrow, and there's still some packing to do."

And that was it. Kate and her mum went back down the path, waving, and Maddy was left on her own.

"I've finished," said Maddy, pushing away her half-eaten dinner. Mum had made her favourite pasta, but she just wasn't hungry.

Her dad leaned over and put an arm round her shoulders. "Do you think we could tell her the news? To cheer her up?" he suggested to Maddy's mum, and she nodded.

"What news?" Maddy sniffed sadly.

"Do you remember me telling you that my friend Donna's cat had kittens a couple of months ago?" Mum asked.

"Oh, yes. You showed me a photo on your phone. They're gorgeous. There were some tortoiseshell ones – my favourite kind!"

"Good. Because one of them is going to be yours!"

Maddy blinked. "I'm getting a kitten?"

"You can choose which of the litter you'd like. Donna needs to find homes

16

for them all, and we thought it would be nice for you to have a cat, as you've wanted one for so long. Especially as you're bound to miss Kate – getting to know a kitten might make the Easter holidays a bit less sad." Her mum looked at her anxiously. "We're not trying to take your mind off missing her, Maddy. It's a really sad thing for a friend to move away."

"It just seemed like a good time," her dad added.

Maddy nodded. "It is a good time," she whispered. She couldn't help still feeling sad about Kate, of course, but at the same time, inside she was jumping about and squeaking. *A kitten! A kitten! I'm getting a kitten!*

Chapter Two

Maddy's mum showed her some more photos of the kittens, but it was hard to see them in the pictures on her phone. Three of them were ginger and the other two were tortoiseshells, beautiful black, white and orange cats. They were all coiled and snuggled around each other and their mother, who was black like Ben. Maddy was pretty sure she would like a tortoiseshell kitten – Tiger and Tom had put her off ginger cats.

"When can I see them?" Maddy asked the next morning at breakfast.

Mum smiled. "I've arranged for us to visit them this afternoon. And if you're sure which kitten you'd like, you can even bring it home today! We can go to the pet shop on the way to Donna's house to get everything we'll need."

As it turned out, they needed an awful lot of things. A basket, Maddy had thought of that. And a food bowl. But she hadn't realized there was so much else. A collar. Grooming brush. Food. Special treats that were good for cleaning kitten teeth. Toys…

They were just about to go and pay for everything when Mum stopped.

"Oh, I'm so stupid! I forgot that Donna said to bring a cat carrier to take the kitten home in."

Maddy smiled. *Home!* She loved the idea of their house being a home for a kitten.

"If you get anything else, we won't have room for the kitten in the car," Dad muttered, but Maddy knew he was only joking.

"Can we go to Donna's now?" she said hopefully, as they stowed all the things in the boot a few minutes later.

Mum nodded, and hugged her. "I'm really excited."

Maddy threw her arms round her mum's neck. "I bet I'm more excited than you."

20

Dad got in the car and tooted the horn at them. "Come on. I'm so excited I actually want to go and see these kittens some time today!"

"Oh, look at them!" Maddy breathed, stopping in the kitchen doorway and staring. The kittens were all asleep in a large basket in the corner of the room. It was by the radiator, and the floor had been covered with newspaper.

"They're doing pretty well with their house-training; the newspaper's just in case they miss the litter tray," Donna explained. "We've been keeping them in the kitchen up till now, but this last week they keep on escaping!"

"How old are they?" Maddy asked. They looked so little. She couldn't believe they were ready to leave their mum.

"Ten weeks yesterday. I bought a book about raising kittens when we found out that Dilly was pregnant, and it recommended keeping them with their mum until then, so she can teach them what they need to know. Also, that way they get to spend more time with their brothers and sisters, and learn how to get on with each other."

"So did you mean for her to have kittens then?" Maddy's dad asked.

Donna sighed. "No, it was a total surprise. We were planning to have Dilly spayed, but we left it too late. As soon as she's recovered from having these, we'll take her to the vet. I love the kittens, but I don't want any more!"

"Are you going to keep any of them?" Maddy asked, as she knelt down by the basket. "I can't imagine how you're going to let them go, they're so gorgeous."

Donna nodded. "I know. I'd love to keep a couple, and it will be sad for Dilly to lose them all, but we only ever meant to have one cat! We'll have to see. Quite a few people seem interested in adopting one." She smiled at Maddy. "But you've got first choice. Your mum booked you a kitten weeks ago!"

Maddy looked up at her mum gratefully. "Thanks, Mum!"

"Well, it seemed like a perfect opportunity – you're old enough to help look after a pet now."

"I'll be really good, I promise," Maddy said. "I'll even clean out the litter tray." She wouldn't mind, she thought, peering into the basket. The kittens had heard their voices, and were starting to wake up. Dilly was watching Maddy carefully, obviously guarding her babies.

One of the ginger kittens popped its head up and stared curiously at Maddy. She laughed, and his eyes widened in surprise.

"Oh, sorry!" Maddy whispered. "I didn't mean to scare you."

All the kittens were awake now, gazing at her with big green eyes. Maddy sighed. "How am I ever going to choose one of you?" she murmured. She hadn't thought she'd like a ginger kitten, but they were cute too – their pink noses clashed with their orangey fur.

One of the tortoiseshell kittens put its paws up on the side of the basket, and nosed at Maddy's hand. Its nose felt chilly and tickly, and Maddy stifled a laugh. She didn't want to make the kitten jump.

"Is this a girl kitten?" she whispered to Donna. She'd guessed that the ginger kittens were boys and the tortoiseshells were girls, but she knew it wasn't always that way round.

"Yes, she's a sweetie. Very friendly, she loves to have her head rubbed."

The kitten looked at Maddy hopefully, and Maddy gently scratched the top of her head. Ben had always liked that. The kitten purred, and turned her head sideways, nestling into Maddy's hand.

"She's lovely," Mum said quietly.

"Could we have her?" Maddy breathed. The kitten was still purring and cuddling up against her hand. She was so little and perfect. Maddy was desperate to pick her up, but she wasn't sure she should.

The kitten solved the problem by clambering over the side of the basket – it was a soft, squashy one, and the sides were so high that she looked like she was trying to climb over a bouncy castle. There was a lot of scrabbling, but eventually she landed on the kitchen floor, looking very proud of herself, and set to work mountaineering up on to Maddy's lap.

"Oooh, claws." Maddy giggled, and carefully scooped a hand under the kitten's bottom to give her a bit of a lift. The kitten finally reached her lap, looking quite worn out by the effort, but she purred delightedly when Maddy made a fuss of her.

"Well, it looks like she wants to be ours too," Dad said, reaching out a finger to scratch behind the kitten's ears. "What are we going to call her?"

Maddy looked down at the kitten, who was busily curling herself into a neat little ball. "See that orange patch on her back. It's completely round. Don't you think it looks just like a biscuit?"

"Biscuit?" Mum laughed. "That's a really cute name for a cat. It does look like a little ginger biscuit, against that white fur."

Maddy nodded. "It's the perfect name for her."

Maddy had the whole of the rest of the Easter holidays to get to know Biscuit, and play with her. Her mum and dad were right – having her kitten did mean she spent less time worrying about going back to school without Kate. She also did a lot of reading – they'd bought a book on cat care at the pet shop, and she got a couple more out of the library, too.

"Did Donna take the kittens to have their first vaccinations?" she asked Mum at breakfast, the day after they'd brought Biscuit home.

Biscuit was sitting on her lap, looking hopefully at Maddy's breakfast. The cereal looked quite like her cat biscuits, she thought, but it didn't smell the same. She reached up, stretching her neck, and sniffed harder. Definitely not cat biscuits, but a very good smell all the same. She put her front paws on the edge of the table, and darted her raspberry-pink tongue at a drop of milk that Maddy had spilled.

It was sweet and cold, and Biscuit gave a delighted little shiver. Maddy was checking her cat book and didn't notice when Biscuit edged a little further forward, and stuck her tongue in the bowl to lap up her leftover cereal. She got in a good few mouthfuls before Maddy spotted her.

"Biscuit! You shouldn't be eating that! Oh, Mum, look, she's got milk all over her whiskers!"

Biscuit settled back on to Maddy's lap, licking her whiskers happily. She liked her food better, but it was nice to have a change…

"Oh dear! I suppose a little bit won't have done her any harm. You'd finished, hadn't you? And yes, Donna gave us the vaccination certificate."

Mum looked in the folder she'd left on the countertop. "She had them done about three weeks ago."

Maddy checked the book again. "Then we need to take her to the vet soon! She's supposed to have the second vaccination three weeks after the first one. And then in another three weeks, she'll be allowed to go outside."

"Actually, yes, that's what Donna's put in this note. She said we should probably have Biscuit microchipped at the same time."

Maddy nodded. Her book mentioned that, too. The tiny microchip went under the skin on the kitten's neck, and it would have a special number on it, so that Biscuit could be easily identified by any vet if she got lost.

"I'll call the vet tomorrow, Maddy. They won't be open on a Sunday."

Maddy nodded. "That reminds me! Can I call Kate, Mum? I have to tell her about Biscuit!"

Luckily, the vet's had a cancelled appointment on Monday afternoon. Maddy wanted to get Biscuit's vaccinations done as soon as possible, so that she would be able to play with her in the garden. She knew that the little cat would love it. She was so adventurous inside the house. She kept climbing things, and she loved to tunnel under Maddy's duvet and then pop out at her.

For the trip to the vet's, Maddy put the cat carrier next to her on the back seat, and Biscuit peered out at her worriedly. She had only been in the cat carrier once, and that was to come to Maddy's house. Were they going back to her old home again? She did miss playing with her brothers and sisters, but Maddy was just as much fun to play with – and she didn't jump on top of her and try to chew her ears, like her biggest ginger brother had done. Biscuit definitely preferred Maddy's house. She let out a miserable wail as Maddy lifted the carrier out of the car – but then she realized that it wasn't her old home they'd come to after all.

The place smelled very odd; sharp and chemical to her sensitive nose.

But at the same time, it was slightly familiar. Had she been here before?

Maddy put the carrier down on the floor, and Biscuit sniffed suspiciously. There were other smells, too. A strange, strong, worrying smell. It smelled like a dog. A dog had visited her old home once, and she hadn't liked it. She shifted nervously inside her carrier. It was coming closer!

Biscuit gave a horrified squeak as a furry face loomed up in front of her carrier. The puppy peered in curiously and nudged the wire door with his nose.

The kitten bristled, her fur standing

on end and her tail fluffing up to twice its size. She hissed furiously at the dog. This was *her* carrier! She lashed her claws at his nose, but they scraped harmlessly down the wire.

"Barney, no!" his owner cried. "Oh, I'm so sorry, I hope he didn't frighten your kitten."

Maddy's mum laughed. "Actually, I think she tried to fight back; she's a determined little thing."

Maddy looked anxiously into Biscuit's carrier. "Are you all right? Sorry, Biscuit, I was helping Mum fill in the forms. I didn't see what was happening." Then she smiled with relief. Biscuit was sitting in the carrier with her tail wrapped smugly round her legs. She wasn't afraid of some silly dog!

Chapter Three

"She's going to miss me while I'm at school," Maddy said worriedly. She had her coat and her rucksack and her lunchbag – and a kitten sitting on her shoulder, sniffing with interest at the rucksack. "It's the first day I won't have been here to play with her."

"I'll be here though," her mum pointed out. Maddy's mum worked part-time at another school, but she didn't go in on Mondays or Fridays. "I'll play with her lots, Maddy, I promise. And your dad's working from home tomorrow. She'll gradually get used to being left. It'll be fine."

Maddy nodded doubtfully. She'd spent the whole holiday playing with Biscuit and fussing over her. Now she just couldn't imagine a whole day at school without seeing her. And without Kate...

"Come on, Maddy. We'd better go."

Maddy sighed and then carefully unhooked Biscuit's claws from her coat. She put her down gently and rubbed her ears. "Be good," she told her. "I'll be back soon."

Biscuit stared up at her. She didn't

understand what was happening, but she could tell from Maddy's voice that she wasn't happy. The kitten gave an uncertain little mew and patted at Maddy's leg with a paw, asking to be picked up again.

"Maddy, now," her mum said firmly, seeing that Maddy was close to tears. She shooed her out of the door, leaving Biscuit all alone in the house.

Biscuit sat by the front door for a little while, hoping that they'd come back, but she couldn't hear any footsteps heading up the path. She was very confused – she just didn't understand why Maddy had gone away. Eventually, she padded back into the kitchen. She had seen Maddy and her mum and dad use the back door, even though she wasn't allowed out of it yet. Perhaps they would come in that way?

She waited for what seemed like a very long time, but no one came in by that door, either. So she wandered through the house, mewing every so often. Where had they all gone? Were they ever coming back? She looked at the stairs for a while, but she still found them very difficult to climb. Maddy had carried her up there a couple of times, but it took her ages to manage a whole flight of stairs by herself.

Sadly, she trailed into the living room, and clawed her way up the purple throw that Maddy's mum had draped over the sofa. It already had quite a lot of little claw marks in it – Biscuit had quickly discovered that the back of the sofa was an interesting place to sit. She sat down, peering out of the window, hoping to see Maddy coming up the front path.

Instead, she saw a large gingery face staring back at her.

Biscuit was so surprised that she jumped backwards with a miaow of fright, and fell on to the seat of the sofa.

What was that? Another cat? In her garden? Biscuit had never been out in it, but she was quite certain that it was hers. She sat shivering on the sofa, not daring to climb up and look again. The other cat had been a lot bigger than she was. What if it was still there? At last, Biscuit scrabbled her way up the throw again, and peeped over the back of the sofa.

The big ginger cat had gone.

Biscuit was so relieved that she curled up on the back of the sofa, and went to sleep.

"She was fine, Maddy!" Mum said, as they walked home from school. "When I got home from dropping you off and doing the shopping, she was asleep on the back of the sofa. And then the rest of the day I fussed over her every so often, and she was perfectly all right."

Maddy nodded, looking relieved. "I wonder if she was watching for us coming home, and that's why she was on the back of the sofa."

"Maybe." Her mum laughed. "Actually, I think she's just nosy. She likes watching people go past. Anyway, how was school?"

Maddy could tell that her mum was trying not to sound worried about her. She shrugged. "OK."

"Who did you sit with?"

"Lucy. And Romany."

"And it was all right?"

"Mmm." Maddy didn't want to tell her mum that she'd felt miserable and lonely all day, and that even though Lucy and Romany had been nice, she'd hardly talked to them. She couldn't help thinking that they were Kate's friends, not hers, and they didn't really want to hang around with her. Luckily it had been netball club at lunch, so she hadn't had to mooch around on her own in the playground. But she didn't have a club every lunchtime. She sped up, hurrying home to see Biscuit.

"Oh, look, she's there, watching out for us!" Maddy beamed. She ran up the garden path, watching Biscuit leap off the back of the sofa. She could hear a little scuttle of paws, and then frantic mewing and a scrabbling noise as the kitten clawed at the door. As soon as her mum opened it, Maddy swept the kitten up to hug her.

School wasn't any easier the next day, or the day after that – but at least Maddy had Biscuit to cheer her up at home. And she was really looking forward to Saturday – the vet had said Biscuit could go out in the garden then, even though it wasn't quite three weeks since her vaccinations. He'd said it would be fine as long as she wasn't around any other cats.

Maddy didn't give Biscuit as much breakfast as usual on Saturday morning. And just in case Biscuit did wander too far, Maddy made sure she had a full bag of the kitten's favourite chicken-flavour treats.

Biscuit was still staring suspiciously at her food bowl, wondering why breakfast hadn't seemed to take as long to gobble down as usual, when she realized that the back door was wide open. She'd seen it open before, of course, but only when someone was holding her tightly, and even then they always whipped it shut before she could wriggle free and go investigating. She crept over to it, keeping low to the ground, expecting any minute that Maddy or her mum would catch her.

But Maddy was outside! She was standing by the door, calling her! Biscuit hurried so fast out of the door, she almost tripped over the step. She shook herself crossly and pattered down the path to where Maddy was.

There were so many smells! She sniffed curiously at the grass, and patted it with one paw. It was cool and damp, and taller than she was!

"Have you got the treats?" Her mum appeared in the doorway. "In case Biscuit goes running off. She could get under the fence if she really tried, remember."

Maddy waved the foil packet. "It's OK. Oh, look, Mum! She's seen a butterfly!"

The orange butterfly was swooping carelessly past Biscuit's nose, and she watched it in amazement. Maddy had dangled pieces of string for her, and feathery toys, but she had never seen anything like this. She reached out her paw and tried to bat at the butterfly, and then tried again with the other paw, but it flew behind her, and she almost fell over trying to chase after it.

"You can't have it, Biscuit," Maddy

laughed. "I don't think butterflies are very good for you. And they're all legs and wings; I bet they don't taste nice."

Biscuit stared after the butterfly, which was flittering over the fence to next door's garden. She thought it looked delicious. But there was no way she could get over the high fence to follow it.

Chapter Four

Maddy and Biscuit spent so much time playing in the garden that on Friday evening, Maddy's dad came home with a surprise. He put the big box he was carrying down in front of Biscuit's cat basket with a flourish.

"What is it?" Maddy asked, peering round to see the front of the box. Biscuit blinked at it sleepily. She was worn out from racing round the garden with Maddy after she had got back from school.

"Oh, a cat flap! Thanks, Dad!"

"We can put it in tomorrow. It's over three weeks since Biscuit had her vaccinations now, so we can let her out on her own."

Maddy nodded. "I suppose so. But she's still not quite fourteen weeks old. She's only little."

"I think cats like to explore though," Dad pointed out. "She'll be able to climb trees. Chase more butterflies…"

Biscuit suddenly perked up, bouncing up in her basket and staring at him, ears pricked. Dad laughed. "You see!"

Maddy had been worried that Biscuit might find the cat flap hard to work, or that she just might not like it – Kate had told her that Ben had taken ages to get used to his. He preferred to have someone open the back door for him. But as soon as Biscuit understood what the cat flap did, she took to it immediately. She spent most of Saturday afternoon popping in and out of it, coming back into the kitchen every five minutes to make sure that Maddy was still there.

Maddy had been a bit anxious that Biscuit might try going into one of the next-door gardens, but even though she'd sniffed at the holes under the

52

fence, she didn't seem to want to crawl through them. There was plenty in Maddy's garden to keep her busy.

Maddy was doing her homework at the kitchen table on Sunday morning, with Biscuit curled on her lap. Her science worksheet seemed to be taking ages. It was probably because she kept thinking about her science lesson on Friday. She'd had to pair up with Sara, a girl she didn't really like, and Sara had kept on making mean little comments throughout the lesson. So now every time she tried to write about the differences between solids and liquids, she just started thinking about how much she missed having Kate to work with. Kate would have said something really funny about Sara, Maddy was sure.

At least she'd seen Becky, one of the girls who sat on the table behind her, making faces at Sara. She'd rolled her eyes at Maddy in an "Ignore her!" sort of way, and Maddy had smiled back.

Now Biscuit yawned and jumped lazily off Maddy's lap, making for her cat flap. She was bored with sitting still, and Maddy didn't seem to want to play. Biscuit had tried chasing her coloured pencils across the table, but Maddy had put them away instead of rolling the pencils for her to chase.

The garden was full of interesting smells, and some bees were buzzing around the lavender bushes. Biscuit watched them, fascinated, her tail tip twitching. She was watching so closely that she didn't see Tiger and Tom sneaking under next door's fence. It wasn't until the two big ginger cats were right behind her that Biscuit heard them creeping through the grass, and whirled round. She was sure it was one of these cats who'd been staring in at her through the window.

The ginger cats had their ears laid back as they snuck towards her. Biscuit backed away from them into the lavender bush. She didn't quite understand what was happening, but she knew the two cats weren't friendly. Her tail bushed out, and she darted a nervous glance towards the door. Could she make a run for her cat flap? But one of the big ginger cats, the one with the torn ear, was between her and the house, his tail swishing from side to side.

Tiger, the one with the darker stripes, was almost nose to nose with her now, hissing and staring. Biscuit was practically squashed into the lavender bush – she couldn't retreat any further.

Tiger cuffed her round the head with one enormous paw, sending her rolling, and Biscuit wailed miserably. What was she supposed to do? Why were they attacking her?

Inside the house, Maddy was still gloomily eyeing her homework. She glanced up as her mum came into the kitchen, looking confused.

"Maddy, can you hear a strange noise? It almost sounds like a baby crying. A sort of howling."

Maddy yelped and suddenly pushed her chair away from the table, racing for the back door. She hadn't been paying attention to the noise, but now she was sure it was Biscuit.

She flung open the door, and Tom jumped round, hissing at her, but Tiger and Biscuit hardly seemed to notice. They were in the middle of the lawn now, and Tiger was about three times the size of Biscuit with all his ginger fur fluffed up. They were making strange wowling noises still, circling round each other. As Maddy watched, Tiger leaped on Biscuit again, and the two cats seemed to roll over and over, twisting and scratching.

"Stop it!" Maddy yelled. She raced over to them, shoving at Tiger, ignoring the hissing and scratching at her hands. She snatched Biscuit up, and yelled at Tiger and Tom, sending them scuttling away under the fence.

"Maddy, are you all right?" Her mum came running out. "It all happened so quickly, I didn't realize what was going on. Is Biscuit hurt?"

"I don't think so, but she's shaking." Maddy carried the kitten inside. "Those horrible cats!"

Her mum sighed. "I suppose they're used to coming into our garden. They think Biscuit's in their territory."

"Well, she isn't!" Maddy snapped. "It's our garden and she's our cat!"

"Yes, we know that, but I bet the cats don't. Give her to me, you need to run your hands under the tap. They must hurt, you're all scratched!"

Reluctantly, Maddy handed Biscuit over to her mum.

"She's so scared," Maddy said, her

voice shaking as she washed her hands. "Tiger's so much bigger than she is. He could have really hurt her." Then she laughed a little. "I saw Biscuit scratch his nose, though, before he ran off."

"Did they go under the fence?" her mum asked. "Is there a hole we could block up?"

Maddy dried her scratched hands and made for the door. "I'll go and see."

Biscuit gave a worried little mew as she saw Maddy opening the door, and Maddy stopped to stroke her. "Don't worry. I'm not going to let those ginger bullies anywhere near you."

She hurried out into the garden, checking the fence. There were holes all the way along – not huge ones, but big enough for a cat to squeeze through.

It was going to be difficult to block them all up. And the fence wasn't that high, either. She was pretty sure that Tiger and Tom could climb it without too much effort.

"What are you doing?" someone asked in a sneery sort of voice.

Maddy straightened up from the flower bed. It was her next-door neighbour Josh, who owned Tiger and Tom. He was a couple of years older than she was and went to secondary school, so usually Maddy was too shy to say much to him. But not today.

"I'm looking at the fence! Your cats just came into my garden and beat up my kitten!" she snapped at him.

Josh shrugged. "Sorry. But cats fight. It's what they do."

"Don't you care? She's terrified!"

"There isn't anything I can do, cats chase each other and they fight. There's loads of cats round here. Your kitten's going to get into fights, Maddy, stop being such a girl."

"OH!" Maddy huffed, and she stomped back inside. Biscuit was not going to fight, because Maddy wasn't going to let any other cats hurt her. She didn't care how scratched *she* got.

But as she shut the kitchen door, slamming it hard enough to set the cat flap swinging, Maddy had a sudden, awful thought.

She could protect Biscuit now, but what about tomorrow, when she went back to school?

"Perhaps we shouldn't have got a cat flap..." Maddy said worriedly.

Her dad scratched his head thoughtfully. He'd been out running when Biscuit got into the fight, and had missed the whole thing. "I can't exactly put that chunk of door back.

Anyway, Biscuit's getting bigger all the time. She won't be such easy pickings for those two next door soon."

"I don't think Biscuit's ever going to be as big as they are," Maddy said. "But it's good for her to be able to go out. She loves being in the garden! Or she did, anyway," she added sadly.

Biscuit hadn't been outside again since the fight that morning. She'd retreated into the dining room. There was a lovely patch of warm sun coming through the glass doors at the back of the room. Biscuit lay in it, feeling the soft warmth on her fur. It made her feel better – not so jumpy and scared.

She stretched out on the carpet lazily and gazed out of the big window through half-open eyes, hoping to spot some butterflies.

Instead, the next time she blinked, Tiger and Tom were there. In her garden, staring at her, just on the other side of the window.

Biscuit's tail fluffed up and she hissed in panic. For a moment, she forgot that there was glass there and they couldn't reach her through it. She was sure that Tiger was about to knock her over again. She raced out to the kitchen and Maddy, mewing in fright.

"Oh! They're back in the garden!" Maddy picked Biscuit up, cuddling her.

Dad quickly filled up a glass that was by the sink and headed out into the garden. But he came back shaking his head. "I was going to splash them –

cats don't like getting wet – but they'd gone already."

"If they keep doing this, Biscuit's going to be frightened all the time," Maddy said anxiously. "It's so unfair."

She was still worrying when she went to bed that night. She'd left the kitten snoozing in her basket in the kitchen, after putting some of Biscuit's favourite chicken crunchies in her bowl, in case she woke up needing a midnight snack.

It took Maddy ages to get to sleep. She tossed and turned, thinking about Tiger and Tom, and then about school tomorrow and how lonely it was going to be. Somehow it all got wound up into her dreams when she finally fell asleep, so that she was sitting doing numeracy with Tiger and Tom (in school uniform) on either side of her. Tiger was just telling her that she was stupid and she'd got her multiplication wrong, when Tom started wowling in her ear. Maddy twitched, turned over – and woke up. That wasn't in her dream – the sound was coming from downstairs!

She flung herself out of bed and dashed down the stairs. The noise was louder now and it was coming from the kitchen. Maddy couldn't understand – it sounded like more than one cat, but only Biscuit was meant to be in there. She shoved open the door, and saw Tiger and Tom by Biscuit's food bowl, gobbling down the chicken crunchies she'd left out.

"Go away!" Maddy yelled. "Out! Bad cats!" Tiger and Tom hissed at her, but hightailed it out of the cat flap. The cat flap – of course. That's how they'd got into Maddy's kitchen!

"What on earth…?" Dad appeared in the kitchen doorway, looking sleepy.

"The cats from next door! They came in through the cat flap, Dad; they were eating Biscuit's food!" Maddy crouched down by Biscuit's bed. She looked terrified, and as Maddy gently picked her up, she could feel how tense the kitten was, as though she was ready to leap out of Maddy's arm and run away at any moment. Her whiskers were twitching, and her little face seemed all frightened eyes.

Mum had been worried that Biscuit might end up making a mess in Maddy's room if she slept upstairs, but Maddy couldn't bear the thought of leaving her on her own.

"Dad, please can I take Biscuit upstairs to sleep with me?" she begged. "I know Mum said she should stay in the kitchen, but she's so scared."

Dad sighed. "I suppose she is very well house-trained now. And she's got pretty good at the stairs, hasn't she?

She'll be all right to come down if she needs her litter tray. I'm going to put a chair in front of the cat flap, in case Tiger and Tom come back."

Maddy nodded. Biscuit was relaxing into her arms a little now, but she was still looking around nervously. Maddy hurried upstairs and fluffed up her duvet into a cosy kitten nest at the end of the bed. It didn't leave much duvet for her, but she didn't mind.

Biscuit stepped cautiously into the warm nest and padded at it with her paws. Maddy was here. She was safe. Tiger and Tom wouldn't be able to come upstairs, she was sure. And if they did, Maddy would chase them away.

Maddy slid into bed and sighed. She'd wanted Biscuit to sleep on her bed ever since she'd got her, but she wished it hadn't happened like this.

Maddy was just falling asleep again when she felt determined little paws padding up her tummy, and a soft wisp of fur brushed across her cheek as Biscuit curled up next to her on the pillow. Maddy giggled. Biscuit's tail was lying across her neck and it tickled.

"We'll sort those horrible cats out," she told Biscuit sleepily. "It'll be OK."

Chapter Five

"Time to get up!" Maddy's mum pulled open the bedroom curtains.

"Mmmm. Oh!" Maddy suddenly remembered that Biscuit was upstairs with her, although she was no longer asleep on her pillow.

"Your dad told me he'd let you bring Biscuit up here. I suppose it isn't doing any harm, as long as you make sure she doesn't get shut in. We don't want her weeing on your bedroom carpet!" She looked around. "Where is she? Has she gone downstairs already?"

Maddy sat up. "She was sleeping next to me."

"She's here!" Her mum was crouching down, peering under the bed. "It's all right, Biscuit, I'm not scary. Oh dear, Maddy, she looks very nervous."

"Maybe she heard you coming in and thought it was Tiger and Tom again." Maddy hopped out of bed to look underneath.

Biscuit was squeezed as far back as she could go, pressed against the wall. Maddy could see her whiskers trembling. "Biscuit! Come on, it's OK."

Very slowly, Biscuit crept out and let Maddy pick her up. But she flinched when Maddy's mum tried to stroke her.

"She's usually so friendly," Maddy's mum said sadly. "Perhaps she'll feel better after some food."

"I hope so." Maddy carried Biscuit downstairs with her once she'd got dressed. She could feel Biscuit tensing up as they came down the hall into the kitchen. She was practically clinging on to Maddy's cardigan, and she didn't seem very interested in eating even when Maddy filled up her bowl.

"Don't worry, I'll keep an eye on her while you're at school," Mum said. "How are things going, anyway?"

Maddy shrugged.

"I know you're missing Kate, but I'm sure there are lots of other people in your class that you could chat to," her mum said persuasively.

But none of them are as nice as Kate, Maddy thought. *And none of them want to chat to me. It just isn't that easy…*

"It's a month till Sports Day," Mrs Melling, Maddy's teacher explained, as she led everyone out on to the school field. "So we're going to be doing some athletics – running,

75

hurdles, relay races, that sort of thing."

Several people sighed grumpily, but Maddy smiled. She loved to run. And she was pretty good at it, too. The sun was shining, and she could feel it on her hair and her arms. She'd been worrying about Biscuit all morning, even though Dad had left the cat flap blocked up, in case Tiger and Tom tried to get in again. Maddy knew Biscuit should be fine, but she couldn't stop thinking about her, and how frightened she'd been. Hopefully some running would shake off the jittery, miserable feeling inside her.

The school field had a big oval track painted on to the grass, and after they'd warmed up, Mrs Melling divided them into groups to run heats. Maddy won her first heat easily – none of the others were really trying – but she was surprised when she beat a couple of boys in the next race. Some of the girls even started cheering for her at the end.

"Well done! You're so quick!" Becky came over and patted her on the back.

Maddy laughed, a little nervously. She'd always liked Becky, but she was really popular and had lots of friends. She was nice to Maddy, but they'd never hung around together much.

"Beat Joe in this last race, please!" Becky begged. "He's so full of himself, look at him!"

Joe was talking to a couple of other boys and doing show-off stretches. He obviously thought he was bound to win.

"OK." Maddy grinned. She wasn't tired at all. As they lined up for the last race she bounced on her toes, staring at the finish line. As soon as Mrs Melling blew her whistle, she shot away, sprinting as fast as she could, and crossed the finish line a whisker ahead of Joe.

"Yay! Maddy wins!" She could hear Becky yelling above all the others. It felt fantastic.

With Becky and the others hugging her and telling her she was a star, it was easy to laugh off Joe growling about girls always cheating. And Becky's table in class was behind hers, so Maddy could see Becky grinning at her every so often as they did their literacy after PE. It was the best time she'd had in school all term. She couldn't wait to tell her mum and dad about it. They kept asking how school was going – it would be nice to be able to say she'd had a fun day.

"How was Biscuit?" Maddy asked hopefully, as she rushed up to her mum after school.

Mum made a face. "She's been scratching the sofa! I had to shut her out of the living room."

"Oh…" Maddy frowned. Biscuit had never done that before. She hoped Mum hadn't been too cross with her.

When they got home, Maddy put her bags down, expecting the kitten to bounce up to her, wanting to play, like she usually did. But Biscuit didn't come running.

"Biscuit!" Maddy looked round anxiously.

"Try upstairs," her mum suggested. "She seems to like it there now."

Maddy ran up the stairs and into her room. She couldn't see Biscuit, but she had a horrible feeling she knew where she was. She knelt down, looking under the bed, and sighed. She was right. Biscuit was curled up in the corner again, looking at her with wide, worried eyes.

"Oh, Biscuit…" Maddy whispered. "It's all right, sweetie, come on out…"

"I don't think we can keep the cat flap blocked up like that," Dad said, looking down at his ice cream thoughtfully. "Biscuit needs to be able to go out."

"But she doesn't want to," Maddy explained. "She's scared."

"It isn't good to keep her in − she should be out sharpening her claws on trees, not the sofa," Mum sighed.

"And it would be nice not to have to keep cleaning out the litter tray!"

"I'll do it," Maddy said quickly. "I don't mind. She's too frightened to go in the garden."

She licked her ice-cream spoon, but she wasn't really hungry any more. She could feel Mum and Dad both looking at her. And she was pretty sure they thought she was fussing too much.

"I think Biscuit might just need to toughen up a bit," Dad said gently.

"She's definitely getting bigger," Mum pointed out. "She'll be as big as Tiger and Tom soon."

"I bet she won't," Maddy said. "And however big she is, there's still only one of her. Tiger and Tom work as a team, Mum! Like wrestlers!"

Her mum frowned, and glanced meaningfully at her dad. Maddy knew what that look meant. They thought she was fussing about Biscuit because of school. Because she was feeling nervous and worried too. Mum and Dad reckoned Maddy needed to toughen up a bit, and make some new friends.

"I'll go and look on the net for some ideas," she said quickly, wanting to get away before they started asking about school again, and if there was anyone she wanted to invite to tea. *But maybe I could ask Becky over?* she thought for a second, and then crushed the idea firmly. Becky was far too popular to want to hang around with her.

"You want to do what?" Josh made a snorting noise.

"A timeshare…" Maddy repeated, wriggling to keep her elbows on top of the fence. She was standing on a bucket to see over the fence and it was a bit wobbly. "You keep Tiger and Tom in some of the time, so Biscuit can go out without them scaring her."

After tea, she'd turned on the computer to search her favourite pet advice websites, and found an email waiting for her from Kate. Maddy had sent her a message a couple of days ago, asking if she had any advice. The timeshare idea was something Kate had read about once, and it sounded perfect.

Maddy took a deep breath. She didn't like talking to Josh; he always made her feel stupid. But she had to. "Please can you think about it? Biscuit's getting really twitchy and nervous. It wouldn't have to be long. Maybe only for an hour a day? Just until she's bigger and she can stand up for herself."

Josh shrugged. "How am I supposed to keep them in? Tiger and Tom have a cat flap. They go in and out whenever they want to."

"But couldn't you—" Maddy began.

"I've got football, I need to go," Josh interrupted. And he disappeared through his back door, leaving Maddy peering over the fence after him.

Maddy sighed. The timeshare had seemed like such a good idea. Except that stupid Josh couldn't be bothered!

She trailed back into the kitchen, and found Biscuit sitting on one of the chairs, staring anxiously at the cat flap – Maddy had moved the chair blocking it so she could get out.

"We'll have to think of something else," she told Biscuit, tickling her under the chin.

Biscuit rubbed her head against Maddy's hand and purred.

She really trusts me, Maddy thought. *I have to sort this out somehow...*

Chapter Six

Biscuit didn't go out on her own at all for the rest of the week. Maddy took her out into the garden a few times, as she was pretty sure Tiger and Tom wouldn't come into the garden if she was there. But as soon as she put Biscuit down, the little tortoiseshell would race for her cat flap. And even when she was inside, she spent most of her time hiding under Maddy's bed. She even weed on the floor a couple of times, which made Mum cross.

"I know it isn't her fault, Maddy," Mum told her on Friday morning, as she scrubbed at the landing carpet. "But the smell is horrible!"

"You don't want us to give her back to Donna, do you?" Maddy asked anxiously.

Mum shook her head. "No… But we need to sort this out. Anyway, we'd better get off to school now."

Biscuit watched them from under the bathroom towel rail. She liked it there. It was warm and dark, and the bathroom didn't have any windows she could see other cats from. She hadn't gone downstairs to eat yet. She wasn't sure she was brave enough. What if Tiger and Tom came back into the kitchen again?

As the front door banged behind Maddy, Biscuit crept out to the top of the stairs. She was so hungry, she would have to risk the kitchen. She hurried down the stairs and peered round the kitchen door. No sign of any strange cats. Gratefully, she hurried in, and started to gulp down her food, stopping every few seconds to glance around worriedly.

About halfway through her bowl, she began to relax a little, and slowed down enough to enjoy the food.

Then the front door banged and she leaped away from the bowl in fright. Was it Tiger and Tom again?

Panicking, Biscuit shot into the corner of the kitchen, trying to hide. She was so frightened that she weed all over the floor.

"Oh, no! Biscuit!" Maddy's mum said crossly, as she got back and saw the mess. "What on earth did you do that for? It's only me." She went to the cupboard under the sink to get some spray and a cloth. "Go on, shoo. I've got to wipe it up now." She flapped the cloth at Biscuit grumpily.

Biscuit was so jittery that the flash of the white cloth scared her, and she shot out of the cat flap to get away from it. Maddy's mum had gone to fetch the mop, and she didn't notice that the kitten had gone.

Biscuit sat on the back step, staring

around the garden. She hadn't been outside for a week, and there were so many tempting smells. And there were bees, buzzing about by the lavender bushes. And butterflies… Cautiously, she padded out on to the lawn, shivering deliciously as the sun hit her fur.

She didn't even see Tiger before he leaped out from under the fence, and spat at her. She turned to race for the cat flap, but he chased her, knocking her sideways and clawing her ear. Biscuit looked around for Tom, wondering if he was about to jump out at her too, but Tiger seemed to be on his own for once. Not that it mattered – he was still more than twice as big as she was and horribly fierce. Biscuit mewed with fright as Tiger pounced at her again. She was never going to be able to get away. Unless… She tried to scratch him, shooting out a sharp-clawed paw, and he retreated a little, hissing. It gave her time to think.

If she couldn't beat him running, perhaps she could go up over the fence? Anything was worth a try. She jumped at Tiger suddenly, clawing him again, and then raced past him, heading for the fence. She scrambled up it, scrabbling and fighting for the top. Then she perched there, wobbling, and looked down at Tiger, who stared back up at her.

Biscuit gave a frightened little squeak, and jumped off the other side of the fence...

"Mum, where's Biscuit? I thought she'd be under my bed, but I can't find her anywhere. I've looked in all the places she usually goes."

Mum frowned. "I haven't actually seen her much today. She weed on the kitchen floor this morning... But I'm not sure when I saw her after that. I had to go and do some shopping, and then I came straight back from town to pick you up."

Maddy looked at Biscuit's bed, as though she might suddenly appear from underneath it. Then she noticed the cat flap. "Oh! You moved the chair!"

"I had to," Mum said grimly. "I was wiping up cat wee round it. I see what you mean though, she might have gone out. But that's good, Maddy! We want her to start going outside again."

"Not if those two thugs from next door are around," Maddy muttered. "I'm going to check outside for her."

But there was no sign of Biscuit in the garden either, even after Maddy called and called.

"Can't you see her?" her mum asked, leaning out of the kitchen door. She was looking slightly worried now too.

"No, and we normally feed her about now."

"I'll look upstairs again, perhaps she got shut in somewhere," Mum said.

Maddy knew she'd already checked everywhere, but she nodded anyway. "Biscuit! Biscuit!" she called again.

"Have you lost your kitten?"

Maddy jumped. She hadn't realized Josh was out in his garden. "Yes, you haven't seen her, have you?"

"Nope."

Maddy sighed. "Could you look out for her? Please?"

"Yeah, all right." But he didn't sound very bothered, Maddy thought.

She ran back inside. "Mum, do you think we should go and look for her? Oh, but we can't!"

"Why not?" Her mum looked confused.

"If your cat gets lost, it's best to leave someone they know in the house – otherwise they might not think it's their home if they come back. My book said so."

"Really? OK, well, if she's not back when Dad gets home, you and I can go and look for her then."

The hour before Maddy's dad got home seemed to crawl past. Maddy kept searching the same places over and over again, just in case she'd somehow missed Biscuit the first five or six times she'd checked.

As soon as she saw her dad at the gate, Maddy was out of the front door and running down the path.

"Biscuit's lost! We're going to look for her, you have to stay here!" she gasped.

Her dad stared at her, and then at Mum, dashing down the path after her.

Maddy's mum looked at him worriedly. "I said we'd go and look round the streets. I don't think she could have gone far."

Maddy was already hurrying down the road, peering under the parked cars. "Come on, Mum!" she called.

Biscuit peered miserably out at the strange garden. As she'd jumped off the fence, she'd been trying to look behind her at the same time, and she'd landed badly, jarring one of her front paws.

It hurt, and so did the scratches. But she'd kept going, desperate to get as far away from Tiger as she could. She'd crawled under fence after fence, hurrying on and on, until at last she felt as if she might be safe. She'd smelled several other cats and even seen a couple, but none of them had chased her yet.

Eventually she'd stopped to rest behind a garden shed. She didn't feel like she could go any further, her paw hurt so much. She'd huddled there for the rest of the day, unsure what to do. She couldn't go home, could she? Tiger would chase her again. She'd have to wait until she was sure Maddy was back, then it would be safe.

They searched for ages. Maddy kept looking at the road and hoping that Biscuit hadn't been so scared she'd run out in front of a car. *I should have taken more care of her. I ought to have made Josh do something about Tiger and Tom,* she kept thinking. *When I find Biscuit, I'm going to tell him!*

They were halfway down the next road and Maddy was hanging over a garden wall staring into some tall flowers, when a surprised voice said, "What are you doing?"

Maddy jumped. She hadn't even

noticed anyone approach. Becky from school was standing behind her, while her mum locked up the car. She was wearing a cardigan over ballet clothes, and peering over the wall to see what Maddy was looking at.

"Oh! Hi, Becky. I'm looking for my kitten." Maddy gulped and swallowed. "She's lost…" It was so horrible to say it.

"Oh no! The cute little tortoiseshell one? You've got her photo in your locker, haven't you?"

Maddy nodded. She was surprised Becky had noticed.

"Want me to help look? Can I, Mum? We were just coming back from ballet," Becky explained. "This is our house. I didn't know you lived so close to us."

Maddy went red. "Sorry about looking in your garden," she said to Becky's mum.

"Don't worry," she replied with a smile. "You can help Maddy look up and down our road, Becky. But only until it's dark – you've probably got another half an hour, that's all."

Maddy looked around anxiously. Biscuit had never even been out at night! She hated the thought of her being all alone and scared in the dark.

The two girls went on up the road, calling for Biscuit, and Becky's mum joined in too, asking their neighbours if they'd seen a kitten. But no one had.

"We have to stop, it's too dark," Maddy's mum said eventually.

"We can't!" Maddy said pleadingly.

"I'll come and help you look first thing tomorrow," Becky told her, giving her a hug. "Don't worry. We'll find her."

At last, as it was starting to get dark, Biscuit decided she could leave her hiding place. Maddy must be home by now. As long as she could get back in through her cat flap before Tiger spotted her, she would be safe.

She crawled out of the dark space behind the shed, wincing as she tried to put her weight on the hurt paw. It seemed to be getting worse. She limped across the garden, and squeezed under the fence, only to see a pair of glinting amber eyes, glaring at her from under a bush. She backed away nervously. Her first thought was that it was Tiger, but it didn't smell like him. It was a strange smell – strong and fierce. And the creature it belonged to was big…

The fox darted forward, and snapped at her, his teeth huge and yellow.

Biscuit ran blindly. She didn't know

where she was going – just away. She darted down the side passage, under a gate and out on to the pavement, where she stopped and glanced quickly behind her. The fox wasn't following. But now she had even less idea where she was, and her paw was throbbing after her panicked dash. She limped on, hobbling down the kerb. She needed to rest, and there was a garden on the other side of the road that looked like a good hiding place, overgrown, with bushes spilling over a low fence. Biscuit set off across the road, not understanding the low growl of the car turning the corner.

She was halfway across when she noticed it – the huge machine that seemed to be towering over her, its lights dazzling her. The car braked sharply, its tyres squealing on the tarmac. Biscuit wailed as she dived forward out of the way, her injured paw collapsing underneath her, so that she half-dragged herself across the road. She struggled through the gate of the overgrown garden and flung herself down under the dark bushes, her breath coming in terrified gasps. She was so tired, and everything seemed to hurt.

Biscuit lay there, gazing into the dark night. She had no idea where she was, or how to get back to Maddy. What was she going to do?

Chapter Seven

Becky's mum dropped her round first thing on Saturday morning. "It's not too early, is it?" Becky asked. "Mum said it might be, but I told her you'd want to get looking straight away."

Maddy half-smiled. "I've been up for ages. I'm just waiting for Dad. It's really nice of you to come."

Becky shook her head. "I said

I would! I want to help you find her."

Maddy's dad appeared behind her. "Ready, girls?"

As they came out of the gate, Tiger and Tom prowled down Josh's front path and leaped on to the wall, staring at them with round green eyes.

Maddy clenched her fists. "Look at them! They're so mean!"

"Are they the ones who scared Biscuit?" Becky asked. Maddy had told her how frightened Biscuit had been.

Maddy nodded. "They're horrible."

Becky pushed open Josh's gate, glaring at the ginger cats. "Come on! Don't you think we should make Josh help us look?"

"I suppose so," Maddy faltered. She shook herself. "Yes, he should."

"Come on then," said Maddy's dad.

Maddy stomped up the path and rang the doorbell hard. She was a bit shocked when Josh's dad answered the front door. She'd been expecting Josh.

"Um… We wondered…"

"Your cats chased her kitten away," Becky put in, over Maddy's shoulder.

Maddy's dad nodded. "She's lost, I'm afraid. We haven't seen her since yesterday morning."

Josh's dad looked worried. "Josh did say something about Tiger and Tom having a fight with a new cat…"

Maddy nodded. "We think they had another fight, and she ran off."

"Oh dear. Look, Josh has got to get to his football match, but can we come and help you look afterwards?"

"Thanks," Maddy told him, and the girls set off to search again.

Biscuit twitched and wriggled in her sleep, then woke up with a jolt, her fur all on end. She stared around the thick bushes, searching for the strange creature that had been chasing her. It had been even bigger than Tiger and Tom. But the gloomy space under the branches was empty – just her and a few beetles. She'd only been dreaming.

She peered out from under the bushes into the overgrown garden, her whiskers twitching.

The house had been abandoned, and the garden was covered in brambles and weeds. Biscuit shivered in the early morning chill. She was stiff all over. She wasn't used to sleeping outside. She hadn't meant to, either, she'd been planning to hurry home to Maddy. But the car had frightened her so much, she'd crawled into this safe little hole and fallen into an exhausted sleep.

Now she had to get home to Maddy. And Maddy would feed her too. She was so hungry, it seemed ages since she'd last had anything to eat.

Biscuit stood up, ready to creep out of her hiding place, but then she collapsed, mewing with pain as her paw seemed to double up underneath her. She'd forgotten. She tried again, putting her

weight on her other front paw, but she could hardly move. She was so stiff, and her injured paw was dragging painfully as she limped through the damp grass. She had to stop and rest every few steps, and her paw was hurting more and more now. Finally, Biscuit sank down at the edge of the weedy gravel path.
She couldn't go any further for a while. She was frozen, her fur was soaked through from the dew, and she was aching all over and so very tired.

How was she ever going to get home?

"If we don't find her soon, maybe we ought to make a poster?" Becky said. They'd searched all down Maddy's road again, and gone round the park, and the maze of little streets between the park and school. Now they were going back down Becky's road.

Maddy swallowed. "Yes," she whispered. It made sense. They'd been searching all morning. But it seemed like admitting that Biscuit was properly lost. Lost Cat posters always made her so sad. She couldn't imagine seeing Biscuit's photo stuck up on all the lamp posts.

"Let's keep calling her for a bit longer," she whispered. She rubbed her eyes to wipe away the tears, then shouted, "Biscuit! Biscuit!"

Curled up by the garden path, Biscuit was startled out of her cold half-sleep. That was Maddy, she was sure! She struggled to get up, but she couldn't stand on her hurt leg at all now. What if Maddy didn't see her? The garden was so overgrown, Maddy might easily miss her. Biscuit wailed desperately, a long heartbroken meow.

On the other side of the road, Maddy stopped suddenly, almost bumping into Becky. "Did you hear that?"

"Yes! Do you think it was Biscuit?"

Maddy's dad came running up the road. "Maddy, I think I heard—"

"I know! We did too! Come on!" Grabbing Becky by the hand, she hurried across the road. "It sounds like Biscuit's in that tangly old garden!"

Becky nodded. "I think you're right. No one lives in that house any more, it's really quiet. And spooky. I don't like walking past it. But it would be a good place to hide if she was scared."

Biscuit could hear Maddy getting closer. She called again, mewing desperately, and scrabbled her way down the path, dragging her useless leg.

"She's here!" Maddy flung the gate open. "Oh, Biscuit, you're hurt! She can't walk, Dad."

"Has she been hit by a car?" Becky asked anxiously.

Maddy picked up Biscuit, as gently

as she could. "I'm not sure. Her paw's hanging a bit funny, but it's not bleeding. She's scratched, though, all round her ears and nose. I knew Tiger and Tom had been after her again!"

"We'd better get her looked over by the vet," said Dad, taking out his phone.

Biscuit lay in Maddy's arms, purring faintly. Maddy had found her. She should have known. She rubbed her chin lovingly against Maddy's jumper. She wasn't leaving her, ever again.

Chapter Eight

"Is she going to be all right?" Maddy asked, exchanging an anxious look with Becky. Becky had begged to be allowed to come to the vet; she was desperate to know if Biscuit was going to be OK.

The vet nodded slowly. "I think she's just torn a muscle in her leg. She probably jumped and landed badly. She just needs to rest it. And I'll clean up these scratches and give her an injection of antibiotics, just in case. You said she's had trouble with the neighbour's cats? Looks like she's had a hard time."

Maddy nodded. "She won't go outside, she's so scared. They even came in through her cat flap. I think that was the worst thing. I'm not sure she feels safe even inside the house now."

The vet glanced at his computer screen. "She is microchipped, isn't she?"

"Yes, we had it done with her vaccinations," Dad said. "Why?"

"There's a new kind of cat flap you can get – it's a bit expensive, but it works off the microchip. So only your cat will be able to use it, you see."

Maddy looked up at Dad hopefully. "Can I have one of those for my birthday, just a bit early? Please?"

Dad was grinning. "Two months early? We might be able to stretch to it."

"You can program it, as well, so you can keep Biscuit in at night, if you like," the vet added.

Maddy nodded. "Then if Josh and his dad agree to keep Tiger and Tom in some of the time, we could tell the cat flap only to let Biscuit out when we know they're inside!"

"Was it two tomcats who were fighting her?" the vet asked. "Are they neutered? Boy cats can be rough, if they haven't been. It might be worth suggesting to their owner that he gets them done. I'll give you a leaflet."

"We'll talk to Josh's dad, Maddy," Dad promised.

As Dad drove back home, Maddy cradled Biscuit in her lap. They'd gone off to the vet's in such a rush, they hadn't had time to put her in her travel crate.

"I'll drop you two off, and then I'll go and see if that big pet shop by the supermarket has those special cat flaps," Dad said, as he pulled in.

"Look, there's Josh and his dad!" Maddy got out, carrying Biscuit.

"You found her!" Josh's dad hurried forward. "Is she OK?"

"She's hurt her paw and we had to take her to the vet," Maddy explained.

"She's really scratched, too…" Josh's dad peered at Biscuit's nose. "Was that our two?"

Maddy nodded. "I think so. Um, are Tiger and Tom neutered? The vet said maybe that would help. He gave us a leaflet."

Becky pushed the leaflet into Josh's dad's hand. "Probably not," he said. "We didn't have them done – they were strays, you see. They turned up at work, about three years ago now, and I brought them home. They were only tiny – about the size of your little one."

"Ohh…" Somehow, knowing that Tiger and Tom had been stray kittens made Maddy feel less cross with them. And Josh and his dad. It wasn't as if they'd asked to be cat owners, and they'd never realized how important it was to have the cats neutered.

"We can try and keep them in sometimes as well, like you said," Josh put in suddenly.

"That would be brilliant," Maddy said gratefully. She brushed her cheek lightly over Biscuit's soft furry head. It was all going to be OK… She should ring Kate to tell her what had happened, she thought suddenly, smiling. It was a nice thought. It didn't make her feel teary, like it would have done a couple of days ago. She missed Kate loads, still. But it wasn't as bad any more, somehow…

"I suppose I'd better get home," Becky said, as they reached Maddy's.

"Would your mum let you stay for a bit?" Maddy asked hopefully.

"That's OK, isn't it?" she added to her mum, who had come to the garden gate and was looking anxiously at Biscuit. "It's good news, Mum, the vet says she's probably just torn a muscle."

"Of course you can stay, after all your help. Ring your mum, Becky. Is she really all right?" Maddy's mum stroked Biscuit gently. "Oh, she's purring."

Maddy beamed. "She is! She must be feeling better, now she's home."

"Maddy!"

Maddy looked round, and saw Becky come racing across the playground. "How's Biscuit?"

"Loads better," Maddy said happily.

"She walking again now. She's got a bit of a limp, but it's not too bad."

"I bet you're fussing over her like anything." Becky laughed.

"I love spoiling her," Maddy admitted. She looked at Becky shyly. "Mum said I could ask you over, so you can see how she is."

Becky beamed. "Really? Yes, please! Can I come today? Just to pop in and see her on the way home?"

"Yes, of course." Maddy could feel her face going pink. She hadn't been sure if Becky would be as friendly at school as she had been over the weekend.

"Do you think Mrs Melling would let you move tables, now that Kate isn't here any more?" Becky asked thoughtfully. "There's space for you to sit with me and Lara and Keri."

"I suppose we could ask," Maddy said, going even pinker.

"Cool." Becky pulled her over to the little group of girls she'd been chatting to. "Have you got a photo of Biscuit in your bag to show everyone?"

"She looks different," Becky said thoughtfully, later on that afternoon as the girls sat in Maddy's kitchen, watching Biscuit sleeping in her basket.

"The scratches don't look as bad," Maddy suggested.

"No, it isn't that. I think she just looks happier. I suppose she must have been feeling really miserable on Saturday." She glanced at the door. "Did your dad get that special cat flap?"

"Yes. And then he went round and worked out the times Biscuit gets to go outside with Josh's dad. He told Dad he'd already rung the vet. Tiger and Tom are booked in for Wednesday. Once they're neutered, the vet said he was sure they'd be less fierce."

"That's amazing." Becky grinned. "Aren't you glad I made you go and ring their bell? Oh look, Biscuit's awake!"

Biscuit opened her eyes and yawned, showing her raspberry-pink tongue.

Then she looked lovingly at Maddy, and stepped out of her basket and on to Maddy's lap. She gave Becky a curious stare.

"Can I stroke her?"

Maddy nodded. "She doesn't seem as jumpy as she did before. It can't really be the new cat flap, because she hasn't even been out yet."

"Maybe she's just glad to be home," Becky suggested.

Maddy smiled down at Biscuit. She seemed to be going back to sleep again, just on a warmer, cosier sort of bed.

Biscuit burrowed deeper into Maddy's school cardigan, and purred softly with each breath. She was safe now. And she wasn't frightened any more.

Also by Holly Webb:

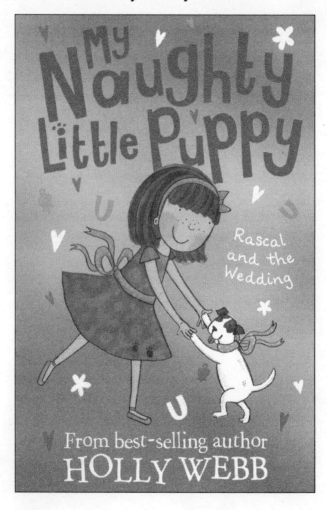

My Naughty Little Puppy

Rascal and the Wedding

From best-selling author
HOLLY WEBB